KATIE WOO
and PEDRO
Mysteries

The Mystery of the Stinky, Spooky Night

by Fran Manushkin

illustrated by Tammie Lyon

WITHDRAWN

PICTURE WINDOW BOOKS

a capstone imprint

Published by Picture Window Books, an imprint of Capstone
1710 Roe Crest Drive, North Mankato, Minnesota 56003
capstonepub.com

Text copyright © 2022 by Fran Manushkin
Illustrations copyright © 2022 by Capstone

Library of Congress Cataloging-in-Publication Data
Names: Manushkin, Fran, author. | Lyon, Tammie, illustrator.
Title: The mystery of the stinky, spooky night / by Fran Manushkin;
illustrated by Tammie Lyon.
Description: North Mankato, Minnesota : Picture Window Books, [2022] |
Series: Katie Woo and Pedro mysteries | Audience: Ages 5–7. | Audience:
Grades K–1. | Summary: Pedro and his dad are walking Katie home on a
foggy night when they are seemingly pursued by something very smelly,
and Katie and Pedro try and solve the mystery of the big smell.
Identifiers: LCCN 2021035332 (print) | LCCN 2021035333 (ebook) |
ISBN 9781663958679 (hardcover) | ISBN 9781666332223 (paperback) | ISBN
9781666332230 (pdf)
Subjects: LCSH: Woo, Katie (Fictitious character)—Juvenile fiction. | Chinese
Americans—Juvenile fiction. | Hispanic Americans—Juvenile fiction. |
Odors—Juvenile fiction. | CYAC: Odors—Fiction. | Hispanic Americans—
Fiction. | Chinese Americans—Fiction.
Classification: LCC PZ7.M3195 Mye 2022 (print) | LCC PZ7.M3195 (ebook) |
DDC 813.54 [E]—dc23
LC record available at https://lccn.loc.gov/2021035332
LC ebook record available at https://lccn.loc.gov/2021035333

Design Elements by Shutterstock: Darcraft, Magnia
Designed by Dina Her

Printed and bound in the USA.   PO4608

Table of Contents

Chapter 1

Feeling Spooked

Katie was at Pedro's house.

"Let's have some fun,"
said Katie. "Let's watch a
spooky movie!"

"That's a great idea,"

said Pedro. "I love movies

with ghosts. Let's watch

The Creepy Haunted House."

"Yay!" yelled Katie.

"Ghosts are the best."

After the movie, Pedro's dad said, "It's getting late. Let's walk Katie home."

Outside, they got a big

surprise. It was foggy.

"Woo-hoo!" yelled Katie.

"Fog is spooky!"

As they began walking,

Pedro said, "I smell

something stinky."

"Me too!" said Katie.

"What is it?"

"I don't know," said Pedro's dad. "It's something we are passing. Soon the stink will go away."

Chapter 2

It Still Stinks!

They walked a little faster.

They passed lots of houses.

The stink was still there.

Then they turned a corner.

The stink was still there!

"This smell is a mystery," said Katie. "But Pedro and I are smart! We will figure out what it is."

"Right!" said Pedro's dad.

"I smell onions," said Katie.

"Me too," said Pedro. "But that's not the smell that is following us. The onion smell is coming from a window."

They walked two more blocks. The stink did not go away.

"I know what it is," said Pedro. "A skunk is following us."

Katie laughed. "Last week, my dog ran into a skunk. I know what a skunk smells like. *Pew, pew, pew!* This stink is not a skunk."

"Let's run!" said Pedro.

"If we run fast, we will get
away from the stink."

Katie and Pedro and

Pedro's dad ran. They ran

far and fast!

Pedro's dad huffed and puffed. "I'm glad I'm wearing my new running shoes."

Chapter 3

Is It a Ghost?

They ran far, but the stink stayed!

"I see something white and wiggly," said Katie. "We are being followed by a stinky ghost!"

Pedro turned and looked.

"It's not a stinky ghost! It's a
bed sheet drying on a line."

Katie giggled. "Boy, did it
fool me!"

"We are not far from your house," said Pedro's dad.

"The worst is over."

But *WHOOPS!* He tripped over a rock and fell down!

Pedro and Katie tripped over him. They got tangled up!

"Yikes!" Katie yelled. "The worst stink is right here."

Pedro began to laugh.

"What's so funny?" asked

his dad.

"You!" said Pedro. "The

stink is coming from poo on

your shoe. *You* are the stinky,

spooky ghost!"

"Way to go," said Pedro's dad. "I knew you could solve the mystery. Now who wants to help me clean my shoe?"

Nobody said yes!

About the Author

Fran Manushkin is the author of Katie Woo, the highly acclaimed fan-favorite early-reader series, as well as the popular Pedro series. Her other books include *Happy in Our Skin*, *Plenty of Hugs!*, *Baby, Come Out!*, and the best-selling board books *Big Girl Panties* and *Big Boy Underpants*. There is a real Katie Woo: Fran's great-niece, but she doesn't get into as much trouble as the Katie in the books. Fran lives in New York City, three blocks from Central Park, where she can often be found bird-watching and daydreaming. She writes at her dining room table, without the help of her naughty cats, Goldy and Chaim.

About the Illustrator

Tammie Lyon, the illustrator of the Katie Woo and Pedro series, says that these characters are two of her favorites. Tammie has illustrated work for Disney, Scholastic, Simon and Schuster, Penguin, HarperCollins, and Amazon Publishing, to name a few. She is also an author/illustrator of her own stories. Her first picture book, *Olive and Snowflake*, was released to starred reviews from *Kirkus* and *School Library Journal*. Tammie lives in Cincinnati, Ohio, with her husband, Lee, and two dogs, Amos and Artie. She spends her days working in her home studio in the woods, surrounded by wildlife and, of course, two mostly-always-sleeping dogs.

Glossary

foggy (FAWG-ee)—covered with a cloudlike mist that makes it harder to see very far

giggle (GIG-uhl)—to laugh in a silly way

mystery (MISS-tur-ee)—a puzzle or crime that needs to be solved

solve (SOLV)—to find the answer to a problem

spooky (SPOO-kee)—scary

All About Mysteries

A mystery is a story where the main characters must figure out a puzzle or solve a crime. Let's think about *The Mystery of the Stinky, Spooky Night*.

Plot

In a mystery, the plot focuses on solving a problem. What is the problem in this story?

Clues

To solve a mystery, readers should look for clues. What are some of the clues in this mystery?

Red Herrings

Red herrings are bad clues. They do not help solve the mystery. Sometimes they even make the mystery harder to solve. What clues in this story were red herrings?

Thinking About the Story

1. Katie and Pedro watched a scary movie. How might that have changed their mood and thoughts for the rest of the story?

2. Did you guess what the stink was before the end? If you were surprised by the ending, what did you think the stink was?

3. Have you ever gotten spooked by something? Write a paragraph about it.

Sniff-and-Go-Seek

In this story, the sense of smell helped Katie and Pedro solve the stinky mystery. Use your sense of smell while playing this fun twist on the game hide-and-go-seek.

What you need:

- a washable object, like a sock or small towel

- a scented spray, like perfume, body spray, or room deodorizer

What you do:

1. Spray the washable object with the scented spray.

2. While one player hides the object, the other players close their eyes and count to twenty.

3. After the object is hidden, the other players search for the object, using their noses as guides. Who can find it first? How long does it take?

Solve more mysteries with Katie and Pedro!

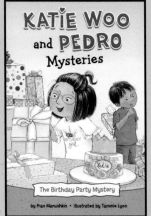

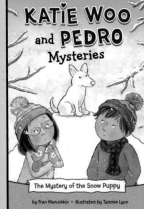

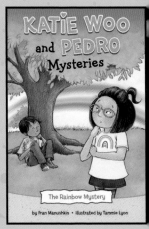